This Mammoth
belongs to

_____

_____

**For
Simon, Bobbin and Tess**

First published in Great Britain 1998 by Methuen Children's Books

Published 1999 by Mammoth an imprint of Egmont Children's Books Limited

239 Kensington High Street, London, W8 6SA

0 7497 3803 0

A CIP catalogue record for this title is available from the British Library

I wish I were a dog

Lydia Monks

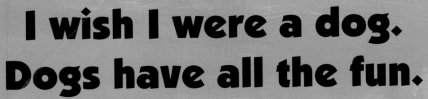

I wish I were a dog.
Dogs have all the fun.

Dogs can play in the park.

Dogs can howl and bark.

They can chase robbers.

They can even be film stars.

I'm fed up!
I wish I were a dog!

**Don't be silly Kitty.
Sometimes dogs are stupid!**

They chew old bones.

They're made to do tricks.

They're put on leads,

and have to do as they're told.

Cats can do lots of things.
Cats are clever.

Cats catch mice.

They can see in the dark,

and move without a sound.

Cats jump high and

cats climb trees.

They can prowl like tigers

and come and go as they please.

**And, of course,
cats can sleep anywhere!**

So you see, you are very special just as you are!